WHEN I TASTED THE JOURNEY

THE STORY OF BEAUTY BEFORE THE FINAL WIN

VEDIKA DORA

ISBN 979-888521666-1

To the ones who have helped me from the time I was born, and are always there for me.

My idols, and my greatest inspiration for this book.

To Mumma and Papa

With Love

- Vedika

Contents

<h1 style="text-align:center;">Preface</h1>

"It's all about the journey not the outcome."
Undoubtedly, Carl Lewis quoted the Truth. Journey is what we all go through. Success is something uncertain. But what is certain is the steps we take. The small steps yet capable of bringing a revolution. Just like a baby on his way to learn to walk, we are on our way to success. We might take the first step and fall on the second. Then two steps, and face failure on the third. Then a few steps, then again a fall. But the journey keeps on going. With that process, one day we end up walking for long time. Now-a-days, do we fall while walking? (I mean, ya there are exceptions, to say a few. But at least not in general.) Now, we have a habit of walking and can continuously walk for as much long as we want. We might get tired, but at least we don't fall while walking. But when we were young, our struggles showed how much difficult it was for us to walk.

In life, what we have learnt so far, is that struggles make our future easier. At present we might feel that this is all so painful or it is going to be impossible. But what we have now with us is our efforts. Nobody thinks before success that this or that day they will be successful. It is just the efforts we make, continuously, day and night, that decides our achievements.

As the title says, I am a foodie. Yes, indeed I am. I love to eat. And that's why the title says," When I TASTED the journey". Jokes apart, In this whole, small and simple story, I have poured my views on what i think is the taste of journey. By taste of journey, i mean to say the experience when we LIVE the journey instead of getting tensed for the success. And believe me, There is no force that can stop you from achieving success once you enjoy the journey.

A self-help in the form of a fiction. A short-story, to say the truth. This is TOTALLY a FICTITIOUS story. Here all characters, their names, the incidents, all are totally imaginary. It is purely a coincidence, if your name matches my imagination. But believe me, I am not a magician or any sort of predictor. Even if you believe, your life matches with the one here, Don't send me copyright strikes. I am INNOCENT.

So, the protagonist - Suvirya Sen, shares her experiences she have earned so far. All throughout the story, i would be delighted if you Imagine yourself as an acquaintance who eagerly wants to know about her life. (She would be delighted too) Sitting in her drawing room. And discussing with her. Once you get the feel, you get the story. So don't forget to Turn on the imagination button and Turn off the nearby disturbances. Tie your seatbelt tightly, as this is going to be a roller coaster full of feelings and enjoyment. Read through with love. From now you will hear from Suvirya.

Over to Survirya

(Imagine yourself as if I pushed you straight into the room, LOL)

Happy Reading!!!

1

Hey There!

Hey, watch out. There's a flower vase behind you. Yes a delicate one. Can you help me change its old flowers and put the new ones... You know life is just like this delicate vase. Not easy to handle. But if handled properly, then there you are - on 'The Top of the World'. Need is to remember to remove the old flowers and to put the new ones. To forget about the past consequences and to focus on the beautiful world ahead.

Life is difficult but not impossible to live. Just a bit hard work, concentration and skills will do it all.

My life is also a journey of a long struggle. From the time I stepped into this world, till now, a struggle-full life is in continuity. But with the passage of time, every single fight with life and for life has given me some great experiences. These experiences not only taught me a lesson but also made me tough enough to face any circumstance. Today I am happy that I suffered from them all, seriously because it is helping me a lot. Just like every strong hit on a metal changes its shape for good, similarly I was changed, and I am still changing for not just my betterment but also for the betterment of the society.

I have a great idea! How about sharing my experiences with people so that they can benefit from it too? Amazing. Instead of going through what I've gone through, Instead of making the mistakes that I made, Instead of taking those bad decisions that had the potential to ruin my life, people can save themselves if they learn from my experiences. After all learning from the mistake of others is indeed a wise man's work.

So, shall we start now? Yes? Alright then. Let us start from the time I was not even born. And we will discuss all my life journey till now. The ups and downs, The goods and bads, The setbacks and the comebacks, The things that tried to break me and the things that made me. All of them. All you have to do is listen and think. It can help you a lot. Lending ears is always like the first aid in any situation. So, tie up your seatbelts and get ready. There we go!!!

2
Flashback...To The Little Me

There's a popular saying. You might have heard people using this sentence - "Impossible says I am possible". This is absolutely correct. Things can be difficult but can never be impossible. For instance, a child of 10 years might find it impossible to solve trigonometry sums. But as soon as he learns the steps, he believes that he can solve them easily now. The only step you need to take to convert any thing from impossible to possible is to remove 'Im'. Look a bit deeper. I said remove 'I AM'. This 'I AM' stops you from doing most of the things. You usually know it as 'EGO' (EGO stands for *Everyone Go Out,* easy peasy). Remove this 'I AM' and That will do everything.

So let's come back to my story. Similarly, My story or better say my journey was difficult But not impossible. This small incident is not just about me but about my whole family who is my biggest teacher. Let us not call this a small incident. It was indeed a greater one which truly had a large impact on me. Let me take you into the past when I was protected by my mother before coming into this world. Here is the incident from my mother's eyes.

She and the whole family was preparing for my welcome into this world. At that time, all of my family members came to know about me. They were informed that I am a small and cute little baby girl. After hearing this news, the so-called people of the society, started quoting things like - "Girls are of no worth", "A boy is the one who can takeover the family", and a million such things. But the thing that had a great impact on me is about to be disclosed. Shockingly but happily too, unlike most of the families at that time, My mother and father were extremely happy and so were my grandfather and granny.

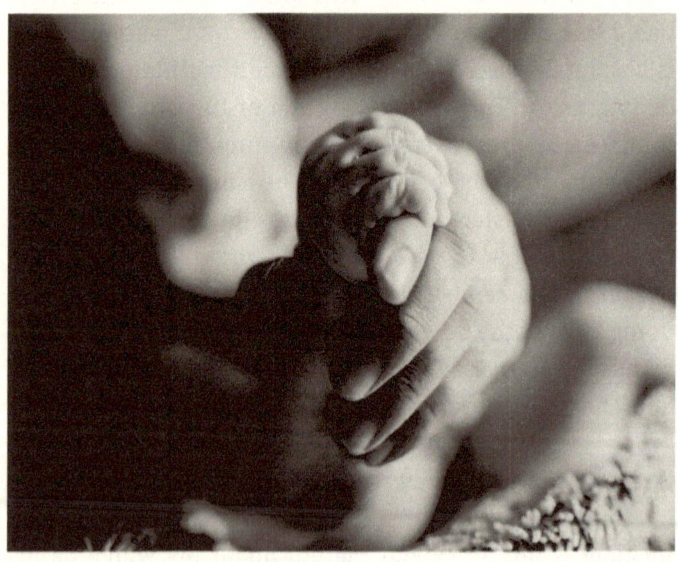

My Granny's first words after my birth were," Thank you God for sending this precious gem to our house".

Grandfather added," Not just a precious gem but also the one who will make us feel proud one day."

My grandpa used to tell me - "When I took you in my arms for the very first time, Your smile made me feel the perfect bliss that one cannot get anywhere else. Your face was shining brightly and the shine made me feel like I have found something I was waiting for since centuries. Your lovely eyes calling grandpa made me the happiest person in the world." He loved me a lot. He tried to be strict in front of me sometimes. Probably to teach me something. But whenever he talked to me, His love poured out from his words and eyes. He have a great hand in making the person I am today.

My grandfather decided to organise a party to celebrate and welcome me into the family. They organised a small 'Havan', or a spiritual ritual, followed by a small party. During the party someone said,"Who celebrates the birth of a girl? A girl is just like a burden, only boys make us feel proud (blah! blah! blah!). Worthless to celebrate the birth of a girl." My grandfather heard this. He said,"Gentleman, I respect your opinion. But we should treat both boys and girls equally."

The person replied, "Why are you behaving like a fool? Men always were the leaders of the society and always will be. Women can never take our place. Treating them equally will never be possible."

"Sir, Today I won't reply you. But I am sure that my granddaughter will definitely shut your mouths one day. That's all I would say."

These words of grandpa influenced me a lot. Whenever I am depressed only these words inspire me to do great.

He further added and announced," She will establish victory against all the negativity of the society. She will prove the people wrong who say that women can do nothing. She will change 'women can do nothing' to 'women can do anything'."

Whatever he said had a lot of depth and it somewhere affected my life in a positive way . The thing that was even more powerful was the reason behind my name. My grandfather was the one who suggested my name.

As my mother told, Grandpa said, "For the elimination of poor thinking, For the establishment of equality and peace and For the victory of good over evil once again, My granddaughter has taken birth. She definitely is a brave hero and will help the people in need. She will become as brave as her name - Suvirya."

Yes. Suvirya. A brave girl who can conquer everything. That's its meaning.

You know in reality, one of the reasons that helped me throughout this beautiful journey was my Grand Pa who believed in me. He said to each one of them with so much confidence that I decided to never let him down. Never ever, for sure. From the time I heard about this incident, I promised that I will, surely, make all his dreams, mine. And that one day definitely I will tell him," Grandpa, I lived the name you gave me, hoping that I made you feel proud."

3

"Little Birdie Flew, But How?"

Before moving forward, let me introduce myself completely along with the area I lived in. I am Suvirya Sen a proud daughter of Mr. Samarth Sen and Mrs. Priyanshi Sen. A blessed grand-daughter of Mr. Vijayendra Sen and Mrs. Ruhani Sen (So many names! Each name has so much power). So this is my family. My support system and people behind my success. They helped me and are still helping me in every way. I belong to a middle-class family. I spent most of my life in a not so developed city. We can call it a developing region, as changes were taking place but at a slower pace.

There were only two schools at that time, one private and the other a government school. The private school was although very much popular at that time. People of different areas used to send their children there. But the school's fees was too high that only richer sections could afford it. On the other hand, the government school was very affordable. But the only problem there was that the girl students were very less as compared to boys. Reason behind this was none other than the thinking of the society which says that boys are more powerful and deserving than girls and girls are made to do household chores. This was the only thing that I wanted to change. So the family decided to send me to the government school.

I started going to school. I don't remember anything about my junior classes, but as my family used to tell me, I was an inquisitive child. Before even going to school, I used to ask several things and was always eager to know about new facts. One such small fact was when I wanted to know HOW BIRDS FLY!

In my garden I played most of the time. There were small plants of *Tulsi* (holy basil), Mint and large trees of Mango and Ashoka. I grew up watching flowers of Hibiscus, Rose, Jasmine and Daisy blooming and shedding and blooming and shedding all over again. I spent most of the time with nature.

One day, a bird came and sat on the edge of the front wall of my house. It was the season of rain and there was mud and water everywhere (it wasn't raining that particular day though). Then the bird sat near me, I saw it and was fascinated by its beauty. I went towards that lovely little creature. Frightened from me, it flew. I asked my mother who was standing near, "Mumma, little birdie flew, but how?" She replied ,"Cause she loves the sky and God loves her; so God gives her the strength to fly." (yes, an explanation to satisfy little child's eagerness)

At that time, I was too small to actually understand its meaning. But today, these words seem so powerful. To know the answer to my question, I started hopping with it. When it hopped, I hopped too. For Sometime, both of us, me and the bird hopped together throughout the garden singing," Chirp, Chirp, Chirp, There we Fly, Fly and Fly! " so lovely it was, aah!

Suddenly the bird flew away. Thinking that God has given me strength, I jumped gathering all my power flapping hands as if they were wings. I wasn't aware about the truth LOL. So, fly and fly and there was I in the mud. Previously, it was mud all over the garden and now it was mud all over me! eww, that was awful.

Grandpa and grandma, who were sitting in the corner of the garden, reading newspaper and enjoying Tea, were gazing upon the scene, laughing on my foolishness. And there I was crying on my situation. Mainly for two reasons. First- it hurted me physically, there were scratches on my knee and one on the elbow started bleeding. Second was that I failed in my attempt to fly. Physical wounds are comparatively easy to treat and overcome than the ones that affect you mentally. Although, both of them can be cured with proper care and love. You may need a little more ointments known as- faith in yourself and some medicines namely determination and will power. At last, they will surely help to cope up with the wound.

This whole incident may be a matter of laugh for some but its true meaning really helped me and can help you out too. This, and many other such incidents too, are evidences of the popular quotation which says -

" Whatever happens, happens for a reason"

My love for the sky of success just like the little bird helped me in achieving my aspirations. I have always observed an eternal bond that I share with birds. Just like they fly high up in the sky, as if it's their goal, to reach different horizons, I also made this my ambition, my goal.

Now what this incident taught me? Firstly that due to my eagerness, I may want to do what is actually difficult. This difficulty may also bring many failures with it,. So I have to be prepared for all of them. Secondly that, on the way to take off my plane for success, I may face defeats, my attempts may not show me sometimes the desired results. But in the end, just like the bird I would be able to fly high and reach the top of success.

This incident which taught me and you one of the great, actually two great lessons of life, looked quite simple on the surface value but had great depth in it. You know, the one who dives deep into the water, is capable of getting the precious gems, not the one who swims near the surface. Similarly in life many events take place. A successful person is the one who goes deep in the depths to take out the valuable lessons, not the one who cries upon his failures. So learn from each and every mistake as they indicate that you are working on yourself.

4
My Mistakes Taught Me!

So, as I told you, I hardly remember anything about my junior classes. But I sill remember the teachers who helped in establishing a base that could support everything in future. They gave me the basic education that is helping me till date. One such teacher was, Sneha Mam. Just like her name, She loved me and my classmates a lot. She used to teach us in a friendly and lovely way. But at times, when someone did anything bad, she used to get really angry. I was a victim of her anger once.

One day, during the school time, Sneha mam was teaching us. I do not remember what she was explaining but we were supposed to write in our notebooks. I was studying in 1st standard, or maybe in a lower class than that. There was a girl sitting next to me. She had a great variety of stationery which everyone used to notice. She wasn't so artistic but had each kind of colors, pencils, erasers and what not. The time mam said to take out our pencils to write, she took out a really beautiful pink-coloured pencil. It had feathers on the top, sparkles on the body, stones all around - In short, everything that can fascinate a child. The pencil was sooooo pretty, aah! Now I thought I must have it. I wanted it at any cost that too immediately. My Good part of the brain was saying -

"You are a good girl, Suvirya. Do what is good, not what is bad. Do, but that thing which does not habe the potential to harm or hurt anyone. Remember, a good child works for the welfare of others, not to bring hardships for them and for yourself too!"

Whereas, Its enemy, My bad brain, was using all sort of 'appealing-to-the-ears' words to convince me. Just like an Angel, Good part tried. But you know what, in the beginning, bad part, or the Devil, seems so attractive, That you cannot ignore it at any cost. Here's what the devil part said -

"Hey! that's a very beautiful pencil. Prettiest of them all. Don't miss out any chance to grab it. Nothing is bad if it makes you feel happy. That beautiful pencil is what you deserve. Lovely feathers, sparkles for a lovely girl. Isn't that make you happy?"

So, both tried to make me believe and follow them with some really convincing points. But I standing like a confused child, at last decided to make myself feel delighted. Yes! I chose the bad part.

I waited for the girl to be busy somewhere else. Suddenly mam called her to give her the notebook she submitted the day before. She went to mam, leaving her pretty-pretty pencil on the desk. This gave me an opportunity. Thinking this to be the right time, I slowly and slowly took my hand near to the alluring pencil, making sure that no one's noticing. YES! I was able to grab it successfully. Then what? Thereit went straight from the desk into the bag in one of the safest pockets. Yeah. I know I did the wrong thing. I succeeded, but will this last long?

I believe whenever I did something wrong in life, Or even if I still do, It always gets corrected with a lesson or two. I mean to say that God always wants me to get mistakes corrected and learn to not repeat them. Thus, every time I do something I was not supposed to, I realise it immediately with my lesson.

Coming back to the story, when she came back to her seat, she started looking worried. Of course anyone would look that way, if he or she had lost something they loved. She started crying suddenly as, the apple of her eye, Her astonishing pink pencil, was lost. And now that she was crying louder and even more louder, The class knew about her. When mam came and asked her what had happened, she explained everything including the appearance of her pencil. Yes, her favourite one. When I took the pencil, I was unknown about one fact that she told to mam.

"The pencil is my favourite (I was aware about it). It was lying on the desk (that's where I picked it from). And - And It was pink in color with feathers and stones (That was what fascinated my senses)", she said, while crying awfully.

" Stop crying, dear. We will find it for you. Just tell me, Anything else you want to share with us about your pencil? It will help us in finding it for you", Mam asked.

"Yes, it had a label. Umm, white colored label with black stripes around it. *Mumma* wrote my name over it."

Oh My God! I never noticed that label. I had plans in my mind that even if mam found the pencil in my bag I would say that my father bought it for me. But now I was in a complete trap. It was obvious that now I won't be able to escape it, AT ANY COST.

"We will try our level best to find your pencil. But have to stop crying, dear." Sneha mam said in the loveliest of her voice that was soon gonna turn ugliest for me.

And that's when the search began. Aunty was called who used to assist mam in numerous works. She was given the duty to find the pencil under and around the benches. Mam, who had a doubt that there must be a thief somewhere among her students, took the job to investigate each and every bag with each and every child. As mam was approaching near, My heart was beating faster. More closer she came, tenser it grew. And then came my turn. I was being checked from top to bottom, each pocket. Nothing found. After all it was in my bag. And then mam started checking the bag. Between the notebooks, In the geometry box, and then the safest pocket (Of course, that I thought was safe enough). She, at last, found The Pencil. clearly written name of the girl in Block letters. I had nothing to say. I was an awfully embarassing moment.

"Was it by mistake or an intentional act? Tell me fast", Mam asked as if she believed that I wasn't guilty. But I, who followed the bad part of the mind, couldn't speak anything.

But being an innocent and truthful child, I spoke and admitted my mistake.

"Sorry mam, I did this intentionally."

And then what? Mam said, oh I forgive you for showing truthfulness, huh? No, not at all. As I said, I faced the angry side, So, *SMACKKK!!!* A tight slap on my face. *Uff!* It was paining and I literally wanted to cry. But I did not cry at that time.

"I didn't expect this from you. Why did you do that?", she asked.

I had nothing to say yet again. I was feeling embarrassed. Is embarrassment a good feeling? Absolutely no, it isn't. Was I going to reply that I loved the pencil and it attracted me to do so? No, how could I? What a foolish reply it would be! But it was the truth Indeed. I chose to remain silent at that time because I had committed a mistake that can't be neglected. I went back home, told whatever happened that day, and promised that I'll never do this again.

What was good in all this was that I learned to not steal anything, that too from my own mistake. I learnt what was wrong and what was right. Another thing that was good here was that my teacher slapped me. Ya, It was painful. But it was pain for the good. If she never slapped and remained friendly everytime, Then I would have done the same thing many times. I would surely have become a thief then. But she did what was right and guided me the right way.

The moral of the story - If you want something, earn it using the right means. Don't try to snatch or steal from others. In this way, it won't be with you lifelong and you will be surely caught in a trap. But when you will earn it, You will have it forever. Not just that, you will also understand its worth. And that will prove to be good for you and others too.

Let's move a little ahead. Have you ever heard about Nelson Mandela. Of course! The person who became first Black president of Africa. He fought against odds especially racism, and established equality, with the help of his people, in Africa. He said a very beautiful thing about fear and courage in one speech.

"I learned that courage was not the absence of fear, but the triumph over it. The brave man is not he who does not feel afraid, but he who conquers that fear."

Absolutely correct without any doubt. All you need is atleast a push. You can not do it all alone (but that doesn't mean that you need to be dependent on someone!). In my case this thing was proved right. All of my fears, in one way or the other, made me an introvert. I shared my thoughts less when I feared. This had the potential to make me weak. Which in future would have been my biggest hindrance. My mom knew about it. And taking the responsibility to help me overcome my fears, she decided to share with me a story. I would be delighted to share the same with you.

Here it is-

It is from the epic Mahabharata. Gandhari, mother of Kauravas, decided to remain blindfolded throughout her life as her husband, Dhritarashtra was blind. She was gifted the boon that whenever she will open her blindfold, the first thing she will see will become like the thunderbolt. This story is about how she used this blessing.

During the Kurukshetra Yuddha (War), many of Gandhari's sons died. In order to save her eldest son, Duryodhana, she called him and described everything about her blessing. She further added and said Duryodhana to come in front of her, totally naked. Not even a single piece of cloth should be there on his body, so that when Gandhari opens her blindfold and sees Duryodhana, he would become totally hard and strong. He agreed and went back.

Now, Shri Krishna heard about it. He said to Duryodhana, that it would be a bad idea to go completely naked in front of a lady. He also suggested that Duryodhana should cover at least the areas around the thighs.

Duryodhana thought that the arguments are reasonable. So, he covered that area and went in front of his mother. He asked his mother to remove the blindfold as he was ready. When his mother did so, she immediately got angry as Duryodhana did not do what was asked. His mother wanted him to be strong from every part. But due to his act, all his body turned hard as stone but the area near the thighs was still soft as flesh. During the war, Shri Krishna knew the truth and helped Pandavas to kill Duryodhana. It was just the attack on that area which killed Duryodhana.

This was the story my mom shared. She then said that I should share each and everything with my parents as they know me better than anyone else do. Just like the situation in the story, our parents know us and when we will share something, they will try to strengthen us. Hiding something will weaken us from that area. She taught me the importance of sharing everything. This incident so simple, but the meaning so symbolic and so strong. It brought great changes in me. It enhanced my personality as I became more strong, learnt to share and discuss my problems and eventually solve them. If this small problem was neglected, then it might have weakened me as a person. That's why, even the tiniest of holes requires a stitch. As a stitch in time saves nine. Consider each of your problem and weakness as an important task to be treated. Otherwise they will have life-long effects. If you have any problem, discuss it, with either yourself, or someone else. It will help you a lot. If you have something important, any advice or suggestion, share it.It will help others too. Sharing is indeed a great thing.

5

The Academic Years

Years passed, and after I completed my 5th class, which is often called the seniormost junior class, I entered the 6th class. Oh My God!! This was so strange (Of course sarcastically). I went through a really great change. Till 5th class, I was so much active in almost everything. From academics to co-curriculars, I used to participate in every competition, every school event, and performed well in exams. I was recognised as a confident child. But it all changed during 6th and 7th class.

We all know that change is necessary. But only if that is a good change and its sole purpose is to bring out the good in you. In this way, it just adds to the profit provided by the necessary change. But in my case the change made me less confident. I started becoming an introvert. Although, academics were going good. Co-curriculars were not even okayish. They were a lot affected. You know, i tried everytime to improve myself. Many times, I failed. The times I got success did not work to improve overall condition as failures were more. Still I managed to pass these two classes too.

Then came, you guessed right, the 8th standard. This was the time, When I was agaist this normal lifestyle. I had two objectives. Number one - Do something different. And Number two - Help others which was and is always my motive.

I wanted to stand out from the crowd. Though I recieved advices that being part of the crowd for girls is good. But my heart never agreed. I know that standing out from the crowd is good but I agree too that it has its own disadvantages. All I dreamt was of not doing what people usually do and at the same time make God and my family feel proud of me.

I used to share this idea with my family, especially my Grandpa. He used to guide me and tell me about the ways through which I can achieve this goal. I still remember the day when he left this world. It was just a few days after my 8th class result. I was happy that at least he saw me fulfilling his dreams, which were my dreams too. I stood first in the whole class, and I remember, I secured 95% then. He was very happy, so was the whole family. He gave me blessings -

"God bless you my little child. May you touch the heights of the success. My blessings are always with you and I am sure that you'll achieve whatever you'll dream. Keep working hard."

He then gave me a tight hug and I said, " Thank you for your loving words. Thank you so much, Grandpa. Be with me forever."

To which he replied, "I am always there with you, here, in your heart forever."

I never knew that these words were indicating something else. Around 3-4 days after my result day, he took his last breath. He was holding my hand that time. His last words, that I still remember, were, *"Shukriya!"* Which means

Thank you. He always taught me to be thankful. Thankful to God, to parents, to teachers, to each and everyone who helped in some or the other way. He taught me that gratitude is wonderful. It has so much power that it can make even difficult things. He taught me to show love and kindness to people all around. Also, he taught me to be tough and strong whenever it is needed and to never bow down to evil. He taught me all the values that life is made up of. I still remember each and everything he said. It gives me the strength to comeback whenever life gives me a setback. He is watching from the heaven and knows how much I love him and that he is always there in my heart.

The Coming Year was tough, however I somehow passed it believing that God and my Grandpa, Both are there with me. My family always supported me and this turned to be a fruitful thing in my case. They helped me at every stage, and are still helping me as I mentioned. They really made me even mre beautiful as a person. Even If I start thanking them for everything, it would take me many such lives to complete. They are the ones who teach you to walk, first physically and later on mentally and socially. They teach you to find your own way to be the best. That is what makes them the best. I love them, more than I love anyone else. They are my strength, my support system. They make my house, a home.

6
The Turning Point - Final

Now, came the real test of life. The Deciding years of my future. 10th, 10+1 or 11th and 10+2 or 12th, (don't think I am teaching you maths, LOL). The classes that form the base for a career. Now that I passed the 10th class, It was time for me to choose a career in which I will be establishing my professional life. As I mentioned before, I wanted to do somethingthat usually people don't do or somethingthat Robert Frost mentioned on one of his poems, 'The Road Not Taken' -

> *"Two roads diverged in a wood, and I*
> *I took the one less travelled by,*
> *And that has made all the difference."*

Though his meaning here is not clear. I am talking about whether he was happy with his decision or not. Because difference can be made two ways, either a good one or a bad one, simple. Though, here he said that his decision of travelling on a unique path made all the difference. I took it in a good way. Travelling on a unique path, knowing that you are on the way that is not a bad one (I hope you are getting my point), this thing in itself is not bad at all. Don't get confused. I simply mean that travelling on a unique path is good. But travelling on the wrong path saying that it is unique, is not good at all.

Okay, so now that I had to choose a path, I chose, Engineering. Yes. I thought that I would be able to complete it with dedication and also no other field provided me the same enjoyment. So, engineering. But in order to pursue it, I would have to complete 11th and 12th with Physics, Chemistry and Maths. The three essentials for any Indian Engineering Aspirant. At first, everything seemed tough. But as they say, practice makes a man perfect. I kept on trying and trying. Honestly, I initially tough of changing my mind. But then I reminded of my young-self and my family. How can I decide to change my field, just because of my fear? Then, I decided to never ever bring such a thought and took it as a challenge to keep going, no matter what. And guess what? Hard work brings to you, the sweetest fruits. Patience and determination, along with hard work and smart work, helped me clear these two classes with flying colours.

One more thing that I forgot to share. My bond with my teachers! Of course, I shared about one of my teachers previously, But that was not it. There were a lot of teachers in my school who loved me a lot. They used to appreciated me and give me a little push every time I seemed to stop on my way. But as you are well aware, there's no rose without a thorn. And the thorn to my seem-so-beautiful journey, were the teachers who criticised me a lot.

One of them, who was my teacher in 7th, used scold me a lot even after I scored amazingly well. And as I mentioned, 7th was the class when my co-curriculars were low and scores were comparatively so good. But still that particular teacher always used to say me, comparing me with other girls of my class, "You can do nothing. Just rush for co-curriculars and make yourself an average student. That's it. No one can make you an excellent student!" And what not. I used to be really depressed that why she always pin points me only.

I am damn sure that there is always a teacher like her in our lives. And you know, eventually she became my most hated teacher. Even after her teaching skills were phenomenal, her way of talking made her the worst teacher for me. I topped my class afterwards too. And she left the school. We never met after that. But you know what this worst teacher actually did good for me. She criticised the way that might be embarassing for a teen, but she made me stronger and I worked hard after that too.

So, many teachers have their most favourites and least favourites. Though a teacher teaches in every way to every student. Still some of us take it the right way, but others the wrong way. That is what makes the difference.

Ya, I passed all those classes and came out as a more confident child. I graduated but then, just like my heart disagreed to do the normal, I again wanted to be unique. I decided to do MBA. So, I did that. And I got a decent job after that (don't ask me for the salary!).

One day when I was on my way to my office, I found a boy who was searching for food. I thought why not I help him. So, I went near him and offered some food. He first hesitated but then agreed. At last, thanking me he said -

"I could have died out of hunger, but because of your help, I survived today. But You know, this doesn't happen every day. I cannot manage to ask for food daily. I want to earn myself but no one gives me a job. I don't want to beg."

His words hit me hard. As a person who got everything from childhood, I can't say that I can understand what he was going through. But I could feel when he said that he wanted to earn and not beg for food.

And then started the Journey of helping others. I took the initiative to start an NGO. Yes, an NGO to help others find there way, especially the ones in need.

As it is being said by Steve Maraboli,

"A kind gesture can reach a wound that only compassion can heal!"

I made my mind to heal every wound with love and compassion. My main aim was and is to help them by not giving money but giving essentials that they can use to earn money themselves. I started daily classes for children, skill classes for adults, so that each one of them can learn and use their potential to earn a living. Besides this, I gave them place to live and food to eat for all the time they were learning those skills. It all started with a gesture a boy did. And here I am Today, in front of you, with a company that offers job to every person in need, who shares the ideas of that boy. The NGO of the people - *A Helping Hand,* soon turned into a place to give employment to them all. I am proud to say that nearly ten thousand people have got their jobs so far, not just here but in great companies too. I couldn't have been more happy than today.

The warmth when you see the smile on their face just changes everything. I am humbled. Happiest moment. Grandpa must be proud too seeing what he wanted me to do.

All this didn't happen in one night. It took years for me to reach here. And I finally feel successful. The most Important thing is that, every incident I shared contributed to this success. It gave me patience, understanding, sense of discrimination, perseverance, hard working spirit and what not. I want you too to learn and share. Contribute to it in whatever way you can and life will truly become exceptionally superb.

7

When I Tasted The Journey...

When I tasted the journey, I found it magical. I found how each incident was success in itself. How every small step contibutes to the big success. This dish was sour, sweet, Bitter sometimes but at last was just perfect.

Throughout my life, I have found one thing that journey is really beautiful, even more when your near and dear ones are with you. Destination is beautiful, no doubt. But the journey has beauty of its own kind. Most of the time, The goal or destination is our point of focus and on reaching it we might experience the perfect bliss. Believe it or not, it would just stay for a few moments. After that it all might become neutral. What matters in reality and is always with us is what we have done throughout our journey. What improvements we have made, what changes we have observed and what new we have learnt, makes the difference. That is why Journey matters more than the destination and for sure is beautiful more than the destination. So focus on the journey and give your best, leave the rest to God. Your hard work will give you the awaited fruits for sure. Have the same attitude for success and failure - the satisfied attitude. Because you are learing in and from both the situations. We need to remeber one thing, always. If we achieve success, we should try to maintain it. And if we face failure, lear to learn from it and give better efforts the next time. That's it.

Journey, as I said, is yummy. It has all the tastes one need or love. Plus, it fulfills the need too. So, its surely a win-win. No matter what comes on the way, YOU WILL SHINE. Remember, your effort matters. When the pencil gets blunt, we first make it sharp and then go ahead. Have a blunt pencil ever stopped someone to not write any further. No! Keep on going. Sharpen yourself whenever necessary.

I hope you get the best. See you soon.

Bye!!!

Thank You

Dear friend,

I thank you from the bottom of my heart for reading this book. I hope it has become your friend, Indeed.

I appreciate you for taking out time. I believe that you have learnt a lot and if each one of us share the word with others and spread the word, Then surely nothing can stop the world to become even more beautiful and peaceful for all. We all fear for the end and no one of us know about the next moment. But what I think is that if we contribute to make others and ourselves feel happy till the end, It won't even matter whether how long we live. As, the length of life doesn't matter but the quality really do.

At last, I would say goodbye with a quote that I love,

"Life is like riding a bicycle. To keep your balance, you must keep moving!"

With love

Vedika